CW00859646

SECRET CORRIDOR

'The hall vanished behind them and darkness closed in. They reached for each other, and their fingers were touching when, with a jerk, the walls stopped moving and they were in utter blackness.

"We have arrived."'

Em and Jay could never have guessed the secret that the apparently antiquated museum was hiding. Why have they been warned off skate-boarding in the wood by a man with a gun? Is it something to do with the brilliant green bird-like flashes they have seen there? Finding the answer proves more and more difficult . . .

Thriller Firsts is an exciting series of fast-paced stories especially for younger readers of the seven to nine year age group. With clear, straightforward text and plenty of illustrations, readers are sure to be gripped.

John Gordon is a popular children's author and this is his first book for Blackie. He has worked as a journalist, before turning to writing full-time.

Other titles in the series

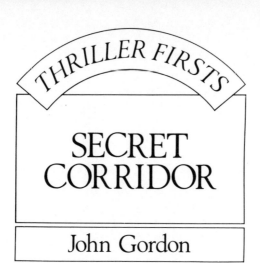

THRILLER FIRSTS

SECRET CORRIDOR

John Gordon

Illustrated by Liz O'Sullivan

Blackie

British Library Cataloguing in Publication Data
Gordon, John *1925* –
Secret corridor.
I. Title   II. O'Sullivan, Liz   III. Series
823'.914   [J]
ISBN 0–216–92986–5

Blackie and Son Ltd
7 Leicester Place
London WC2H 7BP

Printed in Great Britain

1

The Hill

It was the year 2090 and new things were invented every day, but some things never changed. Schools, for instance, and bicycles. Even skateboards. They were just about the same as way back in 1990. The strange birds, however, were brand new.

Nobody was ever quite sure who was the first to see one. Jay always said he'd seen a bright flash of colour in the treetops before they got to the Hill, but Em was sure it wasn't until they were really on the Hill that anybody had seen anything definite. She remembered pointing up and saying 'What's that?' as a brilliant stab of green and blue flickered through the leaves overhead and vanished.

Boris who, as usual, was trailing behind, saw nothing.

However, it was perhaps only a trick of the sunlight, so they had almost forgotten it when they walked along the stream at the foot of the Hill with their skateboards under their arms.

The Hill was their favourite place, and they were lucky to have found it. An old road that had not been used since 1995 snaked down through the trees for almost half a mile, and they had been given permission, just the three of them, to use it as a skateboard track. It was magnificent, but Boris had a grumble.

'I don't see why we have to call at the house *every* time we come here,' he said. The house stood by itself among the trees at the bottom of the Hill, and an old couple called Mr and Mrs Bond lived there.

Em was impatient with him. 'It's *their* hill, and they let us use it,' she said. 'Anyway I like them.'

'I'm hot,' said Boris.

'That's because you're fat,' said Jay.

Em was already crossing the little wooden bridge that led to the bottom of the garden. Mrs Bond was on the other side of the lawn, kneeling beside a flower bed, but she got to her feet and pulled off her gloves. 'I knew you were on your way,' she said. 'I heard you when you were up there.' She nodded towards the slope that rose above the trees. 'There was a tremendous screech.'

'I fell off,' said Em, and dropped her skateboard on the grass.

'And she wasn't even bruised,' said Jay. 'But that's just typical.'

'Well who was it who was too scared to corner flat out?' Em accused him. 'It wasn't me.'

'I had some grass stuck in my wheels,' he said. 'I couldn't get any speed.'

'That's what you say!' Em glowered at him, but Mrs Bond was smiling at Boris.

7

'Who would ever think they were really fond of each other?' she said. She gave a wicked chuckle. 'Oh, dear me, now I've made them blush.'

'They don't ever seem to do anything else,' said Boris. 'Blush, blush, blush — that's them.'

'Now, now, Boris,' said Mrs Bond. 'No teasing.' She wore a bright orange trouser suit which should have been too young for her, but somehow it looked right, even for gardening. She was always so smart that Em often felt clumsy and untidy alongside her, and now Mrs Bond sparkled at her and made it worse.

'You look very hot and sticky, Emma,' she said. Em's name was not Emma. Her great grandmother had been called Emma way back in 1990, but nobody used that name now; it was too old-fashioned. Mrs Bond, however, had to be different. 'Come with me, dear,' she said, 'and we'll freshen up. You two hooligans can cool off in the shade.'

There was a glass table under a striped awning in the corner of the lawn, and a large jug and glasses.

'Drinkies?' said Jay, imitating Mrs Bond. 'Lemonade, I believe, whatever that is.' He knew that people used to drink something called lemonade, once upon a time.

'And what's a hooligan?' said Boris.

'Some sort of goody-goody,' said Jay.

'You mean it's another name for what they used to call a gentleman?'

'That's right.' Ice chinked in Jay's glass. 'Tastes old-fashioned,' he said. 'Like Coke.'

But Boris had picked up his glass and was wandering towards a gap in the long wall that ran all the way down to the stream. 'I heard something,' he said. There had been a sharp whirring sound, then silence.

'It's just one of his windmills,' said Jay. On the other side of the wall there was a vegetable garden where Mr Bond had planted little white wooden windmills he had made to scare the birds away. 'They never seem to work.'

'That's what I mean,' said Boris. 'And there's no wind at the moment, either, so it couldn't have been them.'

'Trust you to notice that,' said Jay with a sigh. 'Why do some people have to be so clever?' But he was curious enough to follow Boris and was just in time to see Mr Bond running along one of the gravel paths between the vegetable plots waving a bamboo cane at something neither of them could see.

'What a weird old man,' said Boris.

Em was upstairs. She had just washed her face and was holding the skin drier up to her cheeks enjoying the faint perfume of the moisturiser it blew gently towards her when something whipped past the open bathroom window and vanished. She looked out.

She saw the two boys as they watched Mr Bond pounding along by the ivy wall waving a stick. But, from above, she could see more than they did. A flicker of bright green was sliding through the ivy like a trickle of water.

Mr Bond stopped, breathless, but after a moment he slowly raised his cane towards a patch of shadow under the leaves. It was then that she saw there was a bird perched there, looking down at him. The tip of the cane got closer and closer, and Mr Bond was making cooing sounds as if to coax it down but suddenly, in a flick of bright feathers, it vanished.

The boys, who had seen nothing, raised their eyebrows at each other.

'Weird,' said Boris.

'Drat the thing!' Mr Bond stabbed his cane at the gravel and turned around. 'Drat the stupid thing!' His rimless glasses glinted as he caught sight of the boys. 'Rabbits,' he said, 'the blasted things get everywhere.'

'On top of a wall?' said Boris, taking a chance.

'Strange creatures, rabbits.' The glasses gleamed, and Mr Bond's thin face became stern. 'I've seen them shin up drainpipes like greased lightning.'

Boris's plump face became quite blank, and Mr Bond smiled. He turned to Jay and said, 'How's the old Ferrari, then?'

'Suspension's a bit sloppy,' said Jay. Mr Bond always gave their skateboards the names of ancient racing cars. Em's was a McLaren, although she'd always thought that had been the name of a toothpaste.

'It just about had me off at the corners,' said Jay.

'We'll get her into the pits and have a look,' said Mr Bond. He stuck his cane into the earth and ushered them towards the lemonade jug. 'Ah,' he said, 'fuel. Time to top up the tanks.'

His thin face was no longer harsh. Cars were his passion. He had an old 1999 Lotus in his garage but wasn't allowed to use it on the roads because it was too fast and too dirty. Cars nowadays were globes of glass that trundled along on four fat little wheels. They ran on electricity, and Mr Bond thought they were so feeble he called them Trixies. He preferred to bike. Which was how they came to meet him one day, cycling along with their skate-boards under their arms.

'And how's Brand's Hatch shaping up?' That was the name he gave to the old road where they raced their boards like 20th century racing cars. 'Track surface still a bit dodgy? Especially at the corners, I expect.'

'And there's weeds all down the middle,' Boris complained.

'But we're going to cut them down,' Jay added hastily. 'If you don't mind, Mr Bond.'

'Feel free, old son. Gardening never was my strong point — which is why it's a wilderness up there.'

'I hope it stays a bit of a mess,' said Jay, and felt Mr Bond's sharp grey eyes on him. 'I mean I'm glad you let us use it.'

'Don't let on, that's all I ask,' said Mr Bond. 'We don't want troops of brats like you out here.' He turned away. 'Ah, the ladies.' He poured a drink for Em and his wife.

'We have just been primping,' said Mrs Bond, 'while you have got yourselves all greasy again, I suppose.'

'Not yet, my poppet. This is just a refuelling

stop.' He winked at the boys. 'But it's always nice to have a pretty bird to chat up at the trackside.'

'I saw you chasing one,' said Em.

'At his age!' cried Mrs Bond.

'No,' said Em, 'I mean a bird-bird, a real one,' and she mentioned the flash of green she'd seen in the ivy.

The smile instantly left Mrs Bond's face. 'I hardly think so, dear,' she said, and she exchanged a glance with her husband.

'But we saw it in the treetops as well.' Em

turned to Jay. 'Didn't we?'

Jay had seen the glance and remembered Mr Bond talking about rabbits. There was something the old man didn't want to talk about. 'I'm not sure it was a bird,' he said. 'Perhaps it was only the sun.'

'But . . .' Em began, and then, just like Mr and Mrs Bond, she exchanged a look with Jay and realised they had both better say no more. 'Well there couldn't be a bird as bright as that around here,' she said.

'About as rare as a climbing rabbit,' said Boris, and everyone laughed, but far too loudly, because there was a secret in the air and nobody was going to mention it.

2

Locked Out

Jay didn't like secrets, but Em thought secrets were all right as long as they were your own. 'It's other people's secrets I don't like,' she said.

Boris believed there might be very good reasons for people having secrets, so he wasn't going to be inquisitive about the birds. 'I didn't see anything, anyway,' he said.

'You wouldn't,' Em retorted. 'But *we* both saw birds, didn't we, Jay?'

'All you two ever see is lovebirds,' said Boris, and had to cycle ahead quickly.

A whole week had passed and school had kept them away from the Hill, but now it was Saturday morning and the sun was shining and they were riding out of town with their skateboards under their arms.

There weren't many Trixies about so they were alone when they came to the gate in the high hedge at the top of the Hill. Em went ahead to open it, but a moment later she turned around and said, 'It's locked.'

'Can't be,' said Jay, but it was. A gleaming chain was padlocked around the post. 'I wonder why they've done that,' he said.

'I knew they would,' said Boris. 'They've changed their minds. They don't want kids around any more.'

'Don't be stupid!' Em cried, and she tossed her skateboard over the gate and climbed after it. Jay went with her and, after he'd thought about it for a while, Boris followed. He heard their shouts as they began the first Grand Prix of the day, and lost sight of them as they plunged down through the bracken to the first bend, but suddenly he stood stock still.

The chain on the gate behind him had rattled. The skin on the back of his head prickled, and he did not want to turn around, but he had to. Very slowly he looked over his shoulder.

The man who leant on the gate wore a brown suit and an old brown hat with a crinkled brim. He was very large and solid and his mouth was hidden by a heavy moustache. He was leaning very comfortably, with his arms

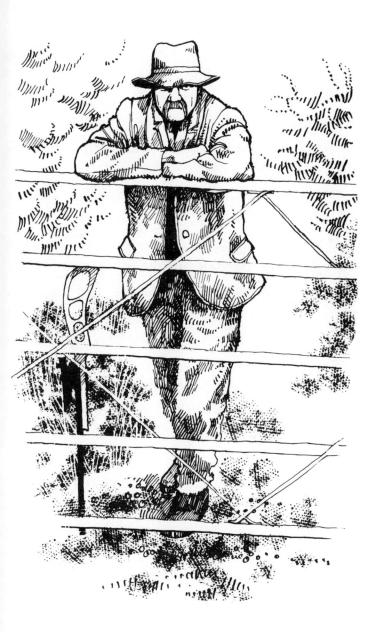

folded, and a shotgun was resting against the bars of the gate. He looked at Boris for a long while before he spoke.

'Where do you think you're going, sonny?' His voice was a deep rumble.

Boris pointed down the slope. 'With them.'

'Well they're not going anywhere. Take a look.'

Boris, not wanting to take his eyes from the man, slowly twisted his head. Jay and Em were struggling back through the bracken while another man waded through the tall greenery behind them. He was driving them in front of him like a sheepdog.

The man at the gate, standing as still as a shepherd, waited until they were beside Boris, and then his voice rumbled at them. 'Are there any more of you?'

It was the man behind them who answered. 'I hardly think so, sir,' he said. He was young and blond, and he was grinning, enjoying himself.

'Let them speak for themselves.'

'Very well, sir.'

It was difficult to see the large man's eyes in the shadow of his hat, but they knew they were being examined.

'Well?' he said.

'We're doing no harm,' said Em.

Jay raised his voice. 'And we've got permission!' He pointed down the Hill. 'Go and ask them.' The young man who stood beside him with a gun in the crook of his arm grinned broadly, and Boris's backbone went cold as the man at the gate shifted his weight and put a hand on the chain.

'This,' he said, 'is a chain, and this is a padlock, and if you listen carefully they say something. They say,' and he added the words very slowly, '. . . Keep . . . Out.'

Jay's mouth was dry, but he swallowed and said, 'This is Mr Bond's hill and he said we could be here.'

The man's moustache hid his mouth and there was not the slightest twitch in his tanned cheeks when he spoke. His voice was quite level, but the knuckles of the large fist gripping the padlock whitened to let them see the huge anger that was building up inside him. 'When

21

I say keep out, sonny, I mean just that.' He spoke very slowly and clearly. 'I don't care what you have been told. You no longer have permission. Understood?'

'But . . .' said Em, and got no further.

'Girl!' The word was roared at her. 'This land is now under my control and you are unwelcome! So get out!'

The grinning man put a hand on her arm, and Jay shouted 'Leave her alone!' but in the next instant his own arm was in the grip of iron fingers and both of them were pushed towards the gate.

The hard eyes under the brim of the hat watched them as they climbed over. He cradled his gun in the crook of his arm, and said, 'Private shooting.' His voice was quite calm again. 'We don't want the game disturbed. Good day to you.' His eyes were on them as they mounted their bikes.

Jay's grandfather had been called Jason, and although nobody used the name now he knew that Jason had been a hero long ago. He had tried to be brave when the man touched Em, but now he was afraid and said nothing.

It was Boris who broke the silence as they cycled away with their skateboards weighing very heavily under their arms.

'Well that's the end of that,' he said riding ahead. 'I told you it was too good to last.'

Jay raised his head suddenly. 'I'm going back!' he said.

'Oh, no, you're not!' Em was alongside him. 'You've done enough already.'

He glanced sideways at her, trying to look into her face to tell what she really thought of him, but the movement made him wobble and he ran into her. They crashed.

Boris stopped and looked back at the scatter of bikes, boards and bodies, and said, 'If you don't move you'll get run over by a Trixie.'

Jay, who was spitting on his knee to get grit out of the cuts, said something so rude to him that Em started to laugh, and Boris said, 'Well if that's the way you feel, I'm going home,' and he rode off.

Which was how Em and Jay found themselves riding into town alone, half-way through a sunny Saturday morning and with nothing to do.

3

The Glass Case

Museum Square had not changed much over the years. Maybe it was cleaner, to judge by old photographs, but it didn't have moving pavements like High Street had now, and it hadn't been roofed over with a glass dome like the Market Place, so it was very much the same as it had always been and people called it part of the Old Town.

The square was quiet and cut off, and it suited the way Jay and Em felt. It stirred something in Em's mind.

'I'd really like to know,' she said, 'what sort of bird that was in the garden.'

'The bird that nobody's supposed to have seen,' said Jay.

'But this is the place to find out,' she said. 'They've got a lot of birds in the museum.'

Jay wasn't keen, but they had nothing else to do so they put their bikes and skateboards into the lock-up racks at the kerbside and climbed the stone steps to the front door.

It was strange to have to turn a handle and push a door, for even doors inside houses only had to be told to open or close and they obeyed (if you said 'Lock', they stayed shut), but not even the doors of the museum had been modernised. It was old and very strange, and not many people bothered with it on a Saturday.

The soles of their shoes squeaked on the polished floor and echoed in the high rooms as though they were being followed by a flock of mewing kittens and Em kept looking over her shoulder.

'I don't like this,' she said. Her mind was still full of what had happened on the Hill, and Jay felt the same. The sunlight was bright outside, but pale blinds had been drawn half-way down the windows so the halls were as cool and dim as deep water.

'They should do something to make this place a bit more interesting,' he said. He kept his voice down so as not to stir too much of an echo. 'Look at all this old stuff.'

The best thing was the inside of a shop with a plastic-fronted counter and an old-fashioned

electronic till, and with clothes for sale such as blue jeans and T-shirts with words and dazzle patterns on the front and back. Em giggled. She wore the newest sort of granny smock, quite short and high-waisted, with embroidered flowers at the hem. She would have liked to try on the old clothes, but she couldn't even touch them because the whole shop was behind glass.

'And that's the most modern thing they've got here,' said Jay. 'No wonder this whole place is empty.' Nobody had entered after them, and every room was silent. They were alone.

Em said, 'Well, I'm glad I'm not a boy because their clothes haven't altered a bit.'

Jay was indignant. 'I'm not wearing anything like those stiff-looking old jeans,' he said.

'Your trousers don't look all that different.' She examined him. His trousers were of thin stuff that never showed a crease and there were no pockets. Like every other man he wore a belt with a wallet.

'And you wouldn't catch me in one of those things.' Jay pointed at a T-shirt with Los Angeles written in silver across the chest. 'Why did they want everybody to know where they'd been?'

She pointed at the open book printed on his sleeveless summer tunic. 'Why do you want everybody to know you can read?'

'Because I can, that's why.' Anyway he always had a book in his wallet.

She put out her tongue at him. 'But I do like the shoes they used to wear,' she said. 'Better than these old see-throughs.' Her own feet seemed quite bare until you picked out the almost invisible transparent straps that held a thin, flexible sole under her foot. She pointed with a toe to the bottom of the glass case and they both crouched to examine a pair of trainers still in their box. Jay thought they looked clumsy, and he was trying to make out just how thick the soles were when he heard Em sigh.

'I know,' he said, 'it's time we were looking at those birds.'

He turned towards her and realised that her sigh had been a gasp. She had drawn back and her eyes were fixed not on the exhibit inside the case but on the glass front itself. And then he saw it, too. There was a reflection in the glass and it was moving. Something was behind them.

They twisted, looking over their shoulders, still crouching. There was nothing. No visitor had come in behind them. They gazed between the legs of the display cases in the centre of the room, and saw nothing but the glass fronts of other displays along the walls.

'But there *was* something,' Em whispered. She was certain she had seen shadows shift.

Very cautiously they stood up. The hall was empty. They could see through an archway into another hall but everything was utterly still.

'Is there somebody around the corner?' Jay raised his voice, determined to show he was not afraid, and he walked towards the archway. 'It must be just another visitor.' He went through the arch, looked to left and right, then shrugged his shoulders. 'They've gone,' he said. 'We're on our own.'

Em smiled back at him as she went towards him. Tall exhibition cases lined the wall ahead of her, and there were even more under the archway. She was glancing along the row, still smiling, when suddenly she frowned.

She was certain that all the tall glass cases had been crowded with stuffed birds, but now one of them wasn't. It was the case right at the end of the row, and it had a curved front because it went around the corner and under the arch. It was like a big bow window, and the exhibit behind the glass was not what she remembered. Instead of birds, the figure of a man stood there.

'That's funny,' she said, and pointed at it.

Jay looked at the life-size figure standing in the centre of the case, one arm resting against the side. The figure was gazing down at a bird that lay in its free hand. 'Something new at last,' he said. 'It's a wildfowler.'

The figure did not look like a wildfowler to Em. It wasn't in shooting clothes, like the man who had chased them off the Hill. In fact, it looked dusty and dowdy, as if it had been there too long. 'I've never seen it before,' she said.

'It's a bit moth-eaten.' Jay went closer. 'It's losing it's hair, and look at its poor old trousers.' He pointed to a torn knee, and then raised his eyes to the rest of the figure. 'His face looks as if it needs a good dust.'

'But his ears are nice,' said Em.

Jay considered them carefully. 'Very life-like,' he admitted. 'A very good quality of ear.'

'You don't see ears like that every day.' Em was laughing. 'They've got nice little twists, can you see?'

They were both leaning forward, laughing, when the figure's dusty eyelids slowly lifted.

'It moves!' said Jay, and he was straining to

see the mechanism that worked it, when a pair of clear blue eyes in the figure's head turned and gazed at him through the glass. And then its mouth opened, and the whole figure stiffened as though surprised.

Jay and Em shrank backwards, stiff themselves, and suddenly cold. A real man stood on the other side of the glass, gazing down on them.

4

The Secret of the Cabinet

The man in the glass looked down on them, and they gazed back. Their hearts thudded and stopped, and thudded again, but for the space of one long breath nobody moved. And then the man did the last thing they could have expected. He turned his back on them.

They began to edge away, but suddenly he turned to face them again and said something. His voice echoed inside the case and was muffled by the glass and they could not make out a word, but suddenly he reached forward and the glass front swung open. He stepped down from the raised floor of the cabinet and stood in front of them.

'This is all very odd,' he said. His long face was puzzled.

'It certainly is,' Jay was surprised at how loud his voice sounded in the big hall. It gave him confidence. 'We didn't know you were there.'

'You weren't supposed to,' said the man.

'That's what is so odd.' He looked quickly beyond them, searching the rest of the hall. 'Is there anybody else?'

Em answered too quickly. 'No,' she said, 'we're alone.'

'Good,' and the man moved quickly for the first time. He tugged at something inside the case and then slammed the glass door and pushed past them. They began to follow but he moved ahead at a trot as he called back over his shoulder something that sounded like 'Lunchtime, I think,' and a moment later they heard his footsteps cross the entrance hall. Then there was the sound of the outer door being locked and bolted and blinds being drawn.

'Now you've done it,' said Jay. 'You've told him we are alone in here.'

'Well, let's get out — quick!' Em was trembling, but they had moved no more than two paces before the man was back in front of them, blocking their way.

'I've shut up shop,' he said. 'Early lunch. Now there's just us.' He stood still, listening. There was no sound anywhere in the museum, not even the buzz of a fly. 'You must have been crouching down over there.' He pointed with the stuffed bird. 'That's how I missed spotting you.'

'If you don't let us leave,' said Em, 'I'll make a noise.'

'What sort of noise?'

'I'll scream.'

'And I'll smash a window,' said Jay.

'Oh, I don't think I can allow that.' His long face looked first at Em and then at Jay. 'You know far too much.'

Em twisted away and drew in her breath to yell. But then she paused. The man had not made a dash at her; he had blinked and closed his eyes. But there was something else. The empty exhibition case was empty no longer. It contained a dead tree with stuffed birds on its branches.

'That was a close thing,' said the man. 'I really thought you were going to scream.'

'I was.'

'So was I,' said Jay.

The man shook his head. 'That would have been very risky,' he said, and looked up quickly. 'And by that I mean risky to me — not risky to you.'

Jay felt his courage coming back. 'I don't see why there's any danger in coming to look at a few old stuffed birds,' he said. 'That's all we were doing,' and he felt Em tug at him and point. Then he, too, saw that the glass cabinet was no longer empty.

'Birds,' said the man. 'Just birds.' The long face was smiling, and suddenly the figure in the dusty clothes with the torn knee seemed dangerous in a different way. He was not going to attack them, but he knew things that nobody else knew. It was the secrets that were dangerous.

Suddenly he reached out and handed the stuffed bird to Jay. 'Hold this,' he said, and he fumbled in his pocket for a key. Then he paused and said, 'I suppose I ought to know who you are.'

They told him.

'And my name is Bond,' he said. 'James Bond,' and he turned away.

'And I'm Flash Gordon,' whispered Jay, who had been watching films that were more than a hundred years old.

The man had not heard him and went on speaking. 'But you can call me what everybody else does.' He was concentrating on putting the key in the lock and seemed to forget he was in the middle of telling them something.

'What do we call you?' Jay reminded him.

'I'm just the museum keeper,' he said, 'so that's what people call me — Keeper Bond, or just Keeper, if you like.' He turned the key, pulled the glass door open and reached inside.

They saw his fingers close over one of the branches of the dead tree, and then he leant back and tugged. There was a lurch and everything inside the cabinet began to revolve. They saw the tree slide by with the stuffed birds trembling on its branches, and it disappeared into a gap that had opened in the back wall. The gap closed and they were staring into a glass case that once more was empty.

'It's a revolving door!' said Jay under his breath. It was the same as any other revolving door except that one section was filled with the display of stuffed birds. 'Nobody could ever tell,' he said.

'Quite so.' The Keeper was pleased, and he stood back to let them step inside.

'Oh, no,' said Em, and shook her head.

The Keeper was puzzled. 'When you say no,' he said, 'do you mean no you won't?'

'Yes — and by yes I mean no — I won't go in there.' She glanced at Jay and saw he was struggling not to laugh.

'I'll go with you,' said the Keeper. 'You're quite safe.'

'What if we don't come back,' said Em. 'Nobody knows where we are.'

The Keeper did not say anything. He reached out, took the stuffed bird from Jay and smoothed its feathers as he gazed down at the floor. He looked so disappointed and sad that Em was on the verge of giving in, when Jay suddenly said, 'Why can't we tell someone where we are? We can just say we are in the museum, and then if anything happens they'll know where to come.' It sounded as if he believed they were about to be murdered, so he added, 'If you see what I mean.'

The Keeper looked doubtful. 'You don't know how important secrecy is,' he said. 'Your parents would want to know too much.'

But Em had an idea. 'We'll only tell one person,' she insisted. 'And we can easily keep *him* from knowing anything, can't we, Jay?'

He knew what she meant. 'Boris!' he said. 'Perfect.'

They made the call in the museum office. The vidiphone showed Boris at home and they mentioned where they were as they told him they wanted to meet him after lunch. He didn't have much to say.

'I think we've hurt his feelings,' said Em as she switched off.

'It's his own fault,' said Jay, but he felt safer now that Boris knew where they were.

The cabinet was large, with plenty of room for three, but when they stepped inside and Keeper Bond turned his back to close the glass door they knew they had gone pale. The door clicked, and as he pushed at the wall and it began to move they shufffled with him into darkness.

5

The Corridor

The hall vanished behind them and darkness closed in. They reached for each other, and their fingers were touching when, with a jerk, the walls stopped moving and they were in utter blackness.

'We have arrived.' Keeper Bond's voice echoed in an invisible space that seemed to be ahead of them in the darkness outside the cabinet. 'Stand still.'

They heard him move away, and Em was clinging with both hands to Jay's arm when there was a faint click and a dim light came on in the distance.

They looked out and saw they were about to enter one end of a very long and very narrow room. There were no windows, and the only light came from the shaded lamp far away.

They could barely see the floor at their feet and they stepped out very cautiously as the Keeper once again swung the revolving door. It swished gently by, and then he said, 'Now the tree is back in position and nobody can tell we're here. Take a look.'

He slid open a little panel which showed a disguised window covered with some gauzy stuff. Through it they saw they were looking out between the branches of the tree into the deserted hall.

'But where are we now?' said Em. The long room they stood in was only a pace or two wide, but now that their eyes were getting used to the dimness they could see that it had tables spaced out along its walls.

'This is where I do my work.' The Keeper went ahead and they followed him into a smell of ancient dust. 'Mind the carpet,' he said, 'it's rather worn.' The long strip of carpet that ran down the centre had holes in it, and the high ceiling was darkened by dust and cobwebs.

'I still can't make out where we are,' said Em.

The Keeper waved a hand towards the wall on the left. 'We are behind the arms and armour gallery,' he said.

'You mean that long room with all the swords and pistols?'

'That's on one side,' said the Keeper, and pointed to the wall on the right. 'And on the other side of that wall is the picture gallery. We are in the middle.'

'But how can we be?' Jay broke in. 'When you're out in the museum there's only the thickness of one wall between those two galleries.'

The Keeper had stopped just short of the shaded lamp that stood on a table half-way along the room. 'Just a single wall between them,' he said, and smiled. 'That's what I used to think — until I started counting.'

'Counting?' Jay was puzzled. 'What did you count?'

'Oh, various things — but however much I counted it didn't add up . . . and that was how I discovered this old corridor.'

'I don't understand that at all,' said Jay, but Em gazed up and down the long room with new eyes. She could see now that it *was* a corridor, a very old one, blocked off. But there was still a puzzle. 'There must have been a door,' she said.

'Way back in the year 2000 there were

several doors,' said the Keeper, 'but they were blocked off one by one by new exhibition cases and this corridor was forgotten.'

'Until you found it.'

'Yes.' He nodded. 'I discovered it.'

'By counting,' said Em, hoping he would explain how he'd done it, but he changed the subject.

'I kept the knowledge to myself,' he said, 'because I needed a place to work without interruption. I installed my own sort of entrance.'

'To keep it secret,' said Em.

'Quite secret,' he said, 'until you two came along.' He looked around. 'The carpet is the one I found here, which is why it has so many holes, I'm afraid — and some of these tables had been left behind, too. It was a kind of time capsule.'

He found that idea amusing and he was still chuckling when Jay bent over to look at some of the objects on the nearest table and said, 'I suppose these old things were here as well, were they?'

'Oh, you are looking at the birds,' said the

Keeper. 'Well I suppose they are old — in a way.'

And then Em, who had been in the shadows, saw them too. Scattered about on the tables, wherever she looked, there were ragged old stuffed birds. Some of them were on perches, but others lay with their claws in the air or with their wings spread out like old finger fans in the dimness. They looked either very lifelike or very deathlike, and she shuddered, but Jay had noticed something else. Tools of all kinds were lying about.

'I suppose you are repairing all these birds ready to put them back in their glass cases,' he said.

'Oh, no.' Keeper Bond was amused. He put the stuffed bird he held into a drawer and shut it. 'I'm releasing them back into the wild.'

Em did not hear him. She could not take her gaze away from the bird that lay nearest the lamp. The light glistened in its eye and it seemed to be looking at her. She had to hug herself tightly before she dared bend closer to examine it. She had no sooner done so than she heard a faint scuffling and drew quickly back.

'There's a mouse on the table!' she gasped. Mice had never made her scream and run, but the thought of a mouse pushing amongst all those feathers was too much. 'It's inside it!' she cried. 'That bird's got a mouse in it!'

Its breast feathers stirred horribly, then one of its claws twitched, and the next moment she did give a scream because by some fluke the bird turned right over and seemed to be hopping closer.

It paused at the edge of the table and then,

in a flash of blue and green, it launched itself straight at her.

6

The Birds

Em jerked back just in time, but the bird's harsh feathers scraped her face and made her cringe away with her hands over her ears as the flutter of its wings filled the air. It beat away down the corridor. She wanted to run but there was nowhere to go.

Then the bird's wings spread wide against the blank wall at the end and it settled on a low ledge. 'Keep it away!' she pleaded, 'Don't let it come near.'

Keeper Bond was apologising to her. 'I'm sorry,' he said, 'that should never have happened,' and he went up to the bird and gently stroked its back. It remained quite still. 'Now it won't be any more trouble,' he said.

A smile wrinkled his long face and he beckoned them forward. They could smell the dust stirred up by the bird's wings as they went towards him, and he switched on another dim light and stood in its glow like a wizard with power over animals.

'What do you think of this?' he said, and lifted a cloth that covered a dome of glass standing on a bench by the wall. Once again Em shuddered, for beneath the dome was what appeared to be a bird's skeleton. It was supported by wires and little clamps as though the glue that held the bones together was still drying.

'Look closer,' he said, and Em held her breath as she bent forward. And then she saw it was not a simple skeleton. Within the bones there was a mass of tiny machinery.

'Clockwork?' she asked.

'Clockwork plus,' said the Keeper. 'Its eyes are solar cells, and there's a microchip or two.'

Jay had put his face right up to the dome. 'And electric motors,' he said. 'Tiny little motors.'

'Of a sort,' said the Keeper. 'More like muscles, I think.'

The little motors had strange shapes. 'I've never seen anything like them,' said Jay.

'Nor has anybody else.' The smile left the Keeper's face. 'That's the trouble,' he said.

Em had not been able to keep her eyes away from the ledge where the bird was still perched. 'But that's not machinery,' she said, 'it's a real bird.' It was preening, splaying out the feathers of a beautiful wing. No mechanical bird would need to do that.

The man unclipped what appeared to be a black pen from his shirt pocket and handed it to her. 'Are you really afraid of birds?' he asked. 'Or were you just startled?'

'Startled,' she said, thinking of her mistake about the mouse.

'Well point this towards it,' he said, and Em

held out the pen at arm's length. 'Now press the tip.'

'Do I have to?'

'I'll do it if you won't,' said Jay, so she pressed it.

Instantly a ray of light shot from the pen and touched the bird. It spread its wings and leapt.

'Stay still!' The man was gripping her wrist when the torch was almost knocked from her grasp as the claws closed on it. The bird shuffled its wings, settled them along its back, and gazed at her with a bright eye. 'It's looking at me!' she said. 'I don't like it.'

'Lenses,' he said. 'Just tiny lenses and solar cells. They are activated as soon as a bright light touches them.'

'That must have been what happened a minute ago,' said Jay, 'when it took off from the bench.'

'Yes,' said the Keeper. He looked at Em. 'It wasn't really flying at you. I'd just let a bit too much light get to it.'

'But it's real,' she said, 'and I don't like feathers!' Touching them made her flesh crawl.

'But these aren't feathers,' he said, 'not real feathers,' and he told Jay to stroke the down on the bird's breast.

'It's cold,' said Jay. 'Not warm at all.'

'That makes it worse!' and Em tried to edge her fingertips away from the bird.

'Metal,' said the Keeper. 'Thinner than silver paper and ten times as strong.'

Jay stroked the bird and found the feathers slip like silk under his fingers. The bird was small, no larger than a thrush, and it was a miracle that so much could be crowded into so small a framework. But it puzzled him. 'Why?' he said. 'What's it for?'

'It's beautiful,' said the Keeper. 'Isn't that enough?'

'But it's got to be *for* something,' Jay insisted. 'It's got to have a *use*.'

Keeper Bond sighed. 'Yes,' he said, 'you are right. When I made it I had something else in mind.' He delicately parted the bird's feathers and they saw what appeared to be a small, circular window.

'It's a camera,' said Jay immediately. 'A

miniature TV camera.'

The Keeper nodded. 'There are still many things we don't know about birds,' he said. 'They are mysterious creatures. So ever since I was a boy I dreamt of being able to fly with them to learn their secrets. This is what I came up with.'

In spite of what he had just shown them, his long face looked so unhappy that Em said, 'Doesn't it work?'

'Oh yes, it works.' He drew in his breath. 'It

works well. In fact it works so well I wish I'd never invented it.'

'I don't see the sense in that,' said Jay.

The man took the perch from Em and gazed down on the bird before he replied. 'My birds aren't always as obedient as this one,' he said.

'I know,' said Em.

He looked sharply at her. 'You know?'

Em glanced shyly at Jay but he, too, seemed mystified. 'We've already seen one of your birds,' she told him. 'We saw someone chasing it, Mr Bond.'

And then Jay's mouth opened wide as he suddenly understood. 'Mr Bond!' he exclaimed. 'And the bird in the garden!' Then the words came tumbling out as they told the Keeper what they had seen.

Keeper Bond ran a hand through his grey hair. 'That other Mr Bond is my father,' he said, 'and he's been helping me to test my birds . . . but they are not yet perfect, I'm afraid.'

'And one escaped,' said Jay.

'And not for the first time.' The Keeper spread his arms and looked around. 'Before I had discovered this place, one of my birds fell into the wrong hands — someone I didn't trust.'

'Couldn't you get it back?'

'I did, in the end, because it got away from him and flew back to me. But he'd seen too much, and he's been seeking for it ever since.' The Keeper looked keenly at both of them. 'Which is why I am forced to tell you all this — and then perhaps you will realise why you must tell no one else.' He waited until they nodded, and then he said, 'That person intended to use my birds for finding out secrets — but not bird secrets. He wanted human secrets because he was . . .'

'. . . a spy!' Jay's mind had raced ahead and he finished the sentence. 'You could find out all sorts of things! Nobody would suspect a bird as real as this. It's great!'

The Keeper's eyes looked steadily into his. 'And would you like to walk in the woods and never know which bird was spying on you? And what about the birds in your garden, or the sparrow on your bedroom window sill?'

Jay was thinking about it when Em made up

her mind. 'I would hate it,' she said. 'Spy birds are horrible.'

'But there are plenty of people who would give a lot for a spy bird,' said the Keeper. 'They can make use of them.'

'Crooks.' Jay could understand that. 'Is that why you told us it was dangerous?'

'Nothing is ever safe,' said the Keeper, and a little smile appeared on his lips. 'I thought my secret workshop was safe until you came along.' He once again rubbed a hand through his short grey hair. 'There is one person who will stop at nothing until he finds where these birds come from. And he already has an idea.'

7

Traitors

They met Boris after lunch. It was a hot day so most of the roof over the Market Place was drawn back and the fountains were throwing handfuls of diamonds into the sun.

They watched a game of chess where the board was set out on the ground like a landscape with hills and woods, and the squares were marked out by streams and hedges where little kings and queens walked in the grounds of their palaces, and where castles were moved by falling into ruin and then being rebuilt in another square whenever one of the players, sitting nearby drinking coffee, pressed a button. Some of the pawns looked like Alice in the old book and it was all very lifelike — 'But not,' said Em after a while, 'anything like as good as the birds.'

'And anyway,' Jay added, 'they're just laser pictures and you can't pick them up like the birds.'

'What birds?' Boris asked, and Jay and Em

were suddenly silent. They had let the secret slip out. 'What are you talking about?' said Boris.

'Nothing much,' said Jay, and turned away, but Em felt guilty. There was no need to be cruel to Boris. 'It's just something we saw,' she told him. 'In a shop.'

'Where?' said Boris, annoyingly

'I can't remember where we saw them,' she lied. 'Can you, Jay?' But Jay shrugged.

Boris looked from one to the other. 'You're not going to tell me, are you?' Neither of them could look him in the eye. 'I thought we were friends,' he said.

'We *are* friends, Boris.' Em turned to him. 'It's just that . . .' and then she didn't know how to go on.

'Some friends *you* are. You want to keep me out of everything just because you're so clever with skateboards and all that stuff.'

Boris was too clumsy to be much good at skateboarding but now he pulled down the corners of his mouth and was so much like a disappointed baby that Em had either to cry or get angry. 'Let's get away from here,' she

said crossly, 'it's too hot.'

Boris trailed behind them looking so miserable that Jay mumbled, 'I wish we could get rid of him altogether.'

Em also wished they could leave Boris behind, but when she looked back and saw him kicking the ground as he walked, sulky and miserable, she had to say, 'But it's not right for him to be so unhappy. It's not fair.'

'Well that's not *our* fault. We can't tell anybody what we know, not even our parents. We promised.'

'Promises, promises – what use are promises if all they do is make someone miserable?'

'Well it's nothing to do with me,' said Jay.

'And sometimes I don't like you, either!' and Em hurried ahead.

They were still strung out, like strangers, when Em realised where she was leading them. In a few moments they would be in Museum Square, and that was the last place they should take Boris. She paused just short of the corner and waited for Jay to catch up.

Boris was behind them on the opposite side of the road when the glinting bubble of a Trixie overtook him and hid him for a moment. It went by, but Boris had vanished. Then they saw him crouching behind a row of other Trixies at the kerbside, and a second later he was crossing the road at a trot, but bent double, with his stomach pressing his knees.

Jay started to laugh but Boris was alarmed. 'Did you see that car?' he said, gasping for breath. They nodded. 'Did you see who was in it?'

The Trixie had turned into the square, and

61

Jay and Em ran the last few steps to the corner just in time to see it back into a parking space and to hear the purr of the four motors inside its little wheels die away. Like all Trixies its front was a glass door tall enough for anyone to walk in without stooping, but the door remained shut.

'Keep out of sight!' Boris was plucking at their sleeves. 'Please! Please! Don't you see who it is?'

'How can I?' said Jay. The sun glinted on the glass door and dazzled him.

'It's that man.' Boris was hopping with anxiety. 'The man with the gun!'

'So what?' but Jay was quickly out of sight with the others.

It was Em who risked a quick peep around the corner. 'He's not getting out,' she said. 'He's just sitting there in front of the museum.'

'He must be keeping watch,' said Jay.

'On us?' Boris was alarmed.

'I doubt it.'

'Who then?'

'How would I know?' Jay was irritable because he was afraid. 'Why don't you stop

asking stupid questions?'

It was then that Boris got his revenge. 'Well if that's where he's going to stay,' he said calmly, 'I know what I'm going to do.'

'What's that?'

'I'm going to take another look at the Hill. That's what. There's something going on there and I want to know about it.'

'That's ridiculous.' Jay tried to sound indignant, but his voice was feeble. 'We'd never find out anything.'

'We might,' said Em, and Jay hated her for

backing Boris.

'And anyway,' Boris's plump face was determined, 'I want to have a word with Mr and Mrs Bond and see what they think about it.'

'We could speak to them on the vidiphone,' Jay said weakly.

'Can't be bothered.' Boris had made up his mind. 'I'll go by myself if you two are scared.' He marched off and they could do nothing but follow.

8

The Marksman

They took the precaution of hiding their bikes in a ditch beside the road before they got to the Hill — 'For a quick getaway,' said Boris, who was enjoying himself too much for Jay.

'Why can't you just shut up,' he said. 'You don't know half of what's going on.'

'Whose fault is that?' said Boris, and Em had to break up the quarrel.

They kept to the stream at the bottom of the Hill, and pushed their way along the overgrown pathway until they came to the wooden footbridge leading to Mrs Bond's garden. The stream barely murmured over its green bed, and all was still.

It was the silence that made them pause and gaze towards the house before they stepped on to the bridge.

'It looks deserted to me,' said Jay. 'I don't think there's anyone at home.'

'There's only one way to find out.' Boris began to move forward but it was Em who put out a hand and held him back.

'I heard something,' she said.

Boris listened. 'No you didn't,' and he was tugging himself free when, across the lawn, he caught a glimpse of bright orange at one of the windows of the house. 'That's her,' he said. 'She's seen us.'

Mrs Bond, in her bright clothes, was at an upstairs window looking out, and she had spotted them even though they were in the shadow of the trees that arched over the bridge. And she was waving.

'Told you,' said Boris, 'and she wants us to go across.'

'No!' Em saw Mrs Bond's hand move, but she wasn't beckoning them closer. She was making a quick downward movement as if trying to push them away or make them hide.

'Don't go!' — but Em was speaking to Boris's back. He was on the other side of the stream when Mrs Bond frantically began pointing, stabbing her finger towards the wall of the kitchen garden.

Jay and Em saw it before Boris knew what was happening. There was a glint of blue and green in the ivy and a bright bird flapped upwards, seeking a perch in the high trees. It never got there. From behind the wall a shot wrecked the silence and the bird staggered against the sky and crossed the lawn in a cartwheeling, shimmering curve to crash ten paces in front of Boris.

'Grab it!' Jay yelled, but Boris was too startled to move. The bird flapped a feeble wing as though fanning itself. Boris took a pace forward, but he was moving too slowly, gazing intensely at the bird, not wishing to go close.

'I'll get it.' Jay leapt on to the bridge, but at that moment there was the sound of heavy footsteps pounding through the paths on the other side of the wall, and Boris turned and ran. He was just in time, for he was on the bridge with Jay when a man with a gun came charging through the gate and pulled up in a slither of gravel as he searched for the fallen bird. His head turned towards the house and he was distracted for a moment by the sight of Mrs Bond at the window. Jay drew Boris further back into the deep shadows of the trees.

Boris could not understand what was happening. 'That bird,' was all he was able to say, and his hand was shaking as he pointed towards it. 'That bird.'

'Keep quiet!' Jay drew him further back, and they were crouching beside Em in the pathway when the man's eyes raked the lawn and saw the bird raise a wing at the edge of the sunshine. He came forward at a trot, the gun held at an angle across his chest and his boots thudding on the grass. It was the young man with the sinister grin.

All three of them crawled quickly into the thick bracken and lay still. They saw him sling the gun on his shoulder and stoop to pick up the bird. He was turning it over in his hands, examining it, when Boris whispered, 'There's no blood. I didn't see any blood,' and then Jay put a hand over his mouth to silence him.

The young man looked briefly around him, smiling slightly just as he had done when he found them on the Hill, and they froze, hardly breathing.

Then he raised his arm and spoke into his wrist-radio. 'Chief!' he said, and waited until there was a tiny answering squawk. 'The spy-bird has landed.' His thin grin broadened as he listened. 'Thank you, Chief. It's just as you told me — camera-eye, motors, the whole shoot.'

He listened again. 'OK, Chief. I'll keep an eye on the old couple till you arrive.' He switched the radio off with his teeth and turned to walk back to the house, ruffling the bird's bright feathers as he went.

9

The Museum Empties

They were pulling their bikes from the hiding place in the ditch before anybody spoke.

'There was no blood,' said Boris. He didn't look at either of them. 'You knew there'd be no blood, but you didn't tell me.'

'We couldn't,' said Jay.

'We promised,' said Em.

He looked at each of them in turn until they lowered their eyes. 'I thought you were my friends,' he said, 'but it seems I was wrong.'

'It's your own fault,' said Jay. 'You should have stayed with us and then you'd have found out.'

'But you didn't tell me,' said Boris. 'You kept it secret.'

'Too bad,' said Jay, and Boris suddenly looked so miserable that Em could stand it no longer. She glanced at Jay.

'You're really horrible!' she said. 'Horrible and mean!'

A sly little smile appeared on Boris's face.

'And I always thought she was really keen on you,' he said.

'Oh, shut up!' Em cried, but she was blushing. 'Shut up, the pair of you!'

She turned away and the two boys looked at each other behind her back. Boris raised his eyebrows and spread his hands as if to say that no one could understand girls, but Jay had seen Em's blush and quite suddenly he realised how pretty she was. But he had to stop Boris saying any more. 'I'll tell him,' he said to her. 'I'll tell him everything.'

He left nothing out, telling Boris every detail, and the more he spoke the more they all realised that dangers were pressing in from all sides.

They were speeding back towards town when Boris said, 'I suppose this Chief feller, whoever he is, is heading out to the Hill right now,' and just as they rounded a bend they saw the glint of a Trixie beginning to climb the long slope towards them.

There was no place to hide, but they were leaning over a field gate looking the other way when it went past. Only Em, between the two

boys, saw the driver. The bronzed face, with its heavy moustache and thick eyebrows, concentrated on nothing but the road ahead as the little car glided by, but Em shuddered. There was no scrap of pity in that solid, silent figure.

They took care entering Museum Square, but there was no watcher and they climbed the steps and went inside. They were not alone; other visitors were wandering through the galleries, and they went straight to the Keeper's office and tried the door. It was locked. They knocked but there was no reply, and they went through the halls but there was no trace of him. There was only one place where he could be, so they went to the glass case and stood in front of it.

'I might believe the rest of it,' said Boris, 'but there's no sign there's ever been a corridor here.' He walked through the archway and gazed along the galleries at each side, and then he turned the other way and looked towards the entrance hall. He was nodding and mumbling to himself.

'What are you doing now?' Jay asked.

'Counting.'

'Counting what?'

Boris shrugged, and Em lost patience with him. 'I don't care what you say,' she said, 'I'll *prove* there's a corridor here.' But then she glanced around and saw there were other people in the hall. 'Count them,' she told Jay. 'Count everybody in the place.'

'What's all this counting?' he said. 'Everybody's doing it.' He remembered that the Keeper had talked about counting, and then there was Boris, and now it was Em.

'Just do it,' she ordered, and she went

quickly out of the hall into the entrance foyer.

There were, in fact, only five people in the museum when they went to report to Em. 'They won't be there for long,' she said, and even before she'd finished speaking a group of three wandered into the entrance hall and went out. She followed them across the hall and quickly bolted the door behind them. 'The important thing is to stop more coming in.'

'You can't do that!' Boris was shocked.

'Oh, can't I?' and she put the sign in the window. 'This museum is closed,' she said, and sat herself on a chair by the door.

'What's going on?' Boris complained. 'Why don't we just wait until the Keeper comes back?'

Before Em had a chance to answer, footsteps came from the direction of the hall and a man and his wife, the last two people, came into the foyer. Em got up from her chair and unbolted the door.

'Oh, is it closing time already?' said the woman.

'I'm afraid so,' said Em.

'But the board outside says we've got another hour.'

'It's an emergency,' said Em.

'Why? What's happened?'

Jay felt his skin prickle, and Boris was already walking away, but Em was smiling up at the man and his wife. 'Mr Bond's father has been taken ill,' she said, 'and he's getting ready to go to see him.'

'Oh, I *am* sorry.' The woman gave her a sympathetic smile. 'And you're his little girl, are you?'

Em smiled up at her sweetly, opened the door, and bolted it behind them. She was so prim, and wicked with it, that Jay was curling up in a corner, choking, but when the bolts shot home the pair of them looked at each other and they suddenly burst into laughter and couldn't stop.

There were still tears on their cheeks when Boris, who had got as far away as possible, came back into the entrance hall. His pale face made their laughter die.

'Someone . . .' he began, and then swallowed and started again. 'Someone was looking at me.' He licked his lips. 'Among those birds in the glass case . . . there's a hole in the back and I saw eyes.'

And then, from the gallery behind him, there came the sound of a door opening.

Em and Jay ran past him and were just in time to see the Keeper step down from the cabinet. He was swinging the tree and birds back into place and he spoke to them over his shoulder. 'Who is he?' he asked. 'Who's that you've got with you?'

They tried to tell him but he hardly listened.

'I told you to tell nobody.' His grey eyebrows were twitching with annoyance, and he suddenly spoke above their heads to Boris behind them. 'Just who are you? And why are you here?'

Suddenly Jay found himself standing up for Boris 'He's with us,' he said. 'He's always with us, and he saw the bird shot.'

'What!'

The angry jerk of the Keeper's head almost made Jay step back. Instead, he went forward a pace and raised his voice. 'They shot the bird. We saw it. It came down right beside Boris and he saw all its works.'

'So he knows.' The fierce eyes flicked to Boris and back to Jay and Em, but his anger faded as they told him about the man with the gun.

'My mother and father,' he broke in, 'are they all right?'

It was Em who told him what the young blond man had said over the radio.

'So,' said the Keeper, and let out his breath slowly, 'they are prisoners.' He closed his eyes and his head drooped forward.

They all stood still, and Em could not stop herself thinking that they were trapped like all the other exhibits around them, the dead birds and the stuffed foxes, who never moved and never would move.

And then the Keeper lifted his head. 'It had to happen,' he said quietly. 'They've got the better of me at last.' He turned to the cabinet and pushed the glass door closed. 'I was in there getting everything ready to take away — but now it's too late.'

'We could help,' said Jay.

'No.' The Keeper shook his head. 'The risk is too great.'

'We could tell someone,' said Em. She was thinking of the police, but he shook his head so violently that she didn't say it.

'They have my mother and father. I will not have them come to any more harm.'

'But . . .'

'No buts.' He began to shepherd them out. 'I want one promise from you,' he said, 'all three of you.' He waited until they had agreed. 'You must on no account give away the secret of my birds — because it is not only my par-

ents you will put in danger if you tell anyone. It is me as well.'

He showed them out of the museum and followed them out into the sunshine, locking the door behind him.

'But what are you going to do?' Em asked.

He gave a grim little smile. 'I think you know,' he said. 'The game is over.'

10

Counting

They watched the Keeper until he went around the corner out of sight.

'It won't take him long to get to the Hill,' said Boris. 'I suppose he's gone for his Trixie. Where does he keep it, behind the museum?'

'How would I know?' Em was cross. 'What does it matter anyway?'

Boris shrugged. They were at the foot of the steps and he was looking up at the front of the museum as if he had something entirely different on his mind. Jay was puzzled by him, so he said 'There isn't any space for parking behind the museum, Boris.'

'Oh is that so?' Boris hardly seemed interested.

'There's just an alleyway, if you really want to know.' He frowned because Boris continued to gaze up at the front of the building. 'And what do you think you're doing, anyway?'

'Counting,' said Boris.

'Not that again! Counting what?'

'Windows. How many are there up there along the front?'

Jay tilted his head and counted the row of windows above the door. 'Seven,' he said. 'So what?'

But Boris had climbed the steps to the front door and was peering through the glass panels. 'Come and take a look.' He beckoned, and they went up and stood beside him. 'You can see into the main galleries from here,' he said. 'How many windows are there at the far end?'

There were three tall windows at the end of each room. 'Six windows altogether,' said Jay.

'Exactly,' said Boris, and Em could stand it no longer.

'What on earth are you playing about at!' she burst out. 'Everything has gone wrong and all you can do is count windows!'

'Come with me,' said Boris, 'I just want to check the figure,' and he walked quickly to the end of the square where they were just in time to see the Keeper's car leave the kerbside and drive away.

'Good,' said Boris, and he walked briskly along the road to where there was a narrow gap between the houses. 'I'd forgotten about this,' he said, and stepped into the passageway.

It was too narrow for them to walk side by side, and grass grew between cracks in the flagstones. 'Not many people come this way,' said Boris. 'Can't blame them.'

They turned a sharp corner and were in a place where no sunlight ever shone. There was a high wall on one side, and on the other a tall building gloomed down on them. Boris stopped and craned his head back, looking up.

'I know we're at the back of the museum,' said Jay, 'but what's the point?'

'Hang on a minute,' said Boris, 'I'm counting.'

Jay looked at Em, raising his eyebrows, but her impatience with Boris had vanished. Everybody, even the Keeper, had talked about counting, and now Boris thought it was important to do some counting in this grimy alleyway. She looked up. Above her head, but out of reach, the back wall of the museum was pierced by tall windows.

Boris had seen her raise her eyes. 'How

many?' he said.

She counted the window ledges. 'Seven,' she said, and Boris turned to Jay. 'And how many windows were there in the galleries?'

'Six.'

'Exactly,' said Boris. 'There's an extra one in the middle. And it shouldn't be there.'

At last Jay understood him. The centre window must be at the end of the corridor between the two galleries.

'I thought it was worth checking,' said Boris, pleased with himself.

'That's brilliant!' said Em, and looked at Jay but he did not seem impressed.

'The only trouble is,' said Jay, 'there isn't a window in the corridor.'

They stood back as far as they could and looked up at the windows. Through six of them they caught a glimpse of the gallery ceilings, but the one in the centre was dark.

'Shutters,' said Em. 'It's got shutters inside.'

'I saw that,' said Boris, 'but it still shouldn't be impossible.'

'What isn't impossible?'

'Well, the Keeper said he wanted to clear some of the things away, but he didn't have time, so I thought we could maybe do some of it for him . . . if we can get inside.'

'But we couldn't . . . we can't . . . we mustn't.'

Jay heard Em stammering and knew he had to act now or he'd never do anything brave again. 'If we can remove some of the things,' he said, 'it might give him a chance to do something. Lean against the wall, Boris.' He pushed Boris into position. 'I'm going to stand

85

on your shoulders.'

It wasn't easy, but with Em's help and reaching up to the window ledge, he managed it. Then his feet were on the ledge and his chin was level with the window catch. He shook the window and it rattled, but would not budge. He reached around to his wallet and pulled out the book that Em had teased him about.

'What are you going to do?' she hissed from below.

'Is anybody coming?' He twisted to look along the alley.

'No,' they said.

He knew there were no windows opposite to overlook him, so he put his toes to the very edge of the ledge, leaned into the window as far as he could, opened the book and put it flat against the glass. Then he punched it, hard.

The crack was muffled but bits of glass went tinkling down inside and the book went with them. He reached through the broken pane and pushed at the catch. It was old and it would not budge until Boris went scouting along the alley and found a loose brick which he handed up.

The catch gave way to Jay's battering, and the ancient paint must also have been loosened because the window slid up. Panting, he pushed at the shutters. They rattled, but would not give.

'They're bolted on the other side,' he said.

'Give 'em a kick.'

Jay looked down at the plump face. 'It's all right for you,' he said. 'It's me who gets caught.'

'We'll keep watch,' and Boris and Em went opposite ways along the alley.

Jay stood on the ledge, gripped the bottom of the window frame with both hands, and kicked. Something clattered to the floor on the other side. He kicked again, the shutters bulged inwards and something splintered. Once more, and a section swung back into the darkness.

They saw Jay ease himself inside but they did not feel the feathers that brushed against him in the corridor or hear the soft thud as a bird fell to the floor. His skin crawled at the touch of unseen things, but he leant out over the ledge and hauled Em up from the step-

pingstone of Boris's back. Then both leant out together and each of them grabbed one of Boris's wrists and heaved.

Boris kicked at the wall, trying to get a toe-hold, and then he had one arm over the sill and Jay got a grip on the seat of his trousers. 'There's not much slack,' he said, 'you're too fat.' Boris came tumbling in over the ledge and fell with such a soft thud on the floor that Jay laughed.

'When you've finished,' said Boris's voice from the floor, 'you'd better get those shutters closed. Something's happening in here.'

Em already knew it. The light from the half-open shutters hardly reached to the end of the corridor, and in the darkness far away there was a stirring and a rustling as if twenty hooded ghosts were scraping their dry feet through the dust towards them.

'The shutter!' Boris cried. 'Cut out the light!'

Jay swung them closed and all three were trapped in utter darkness. They held their breath. The shuffling at the far end fell to a whisper and died.

'What is it?' Em's voice could hardly be heard.

'I would have thought you two would have known.' Boris sounded confident. 'Where's the light switch?'

Jay ran his hand along a table until he came to one of the shaded lamps and switched it on. It was very dim.

'That's more like it,' said Boris. He moved away, not seeming at all afraid, but amazed at everything he saw. 'Marvellous!' he said. 'Wonderful! I'd love a place like this.'

'Be careful!' Em called from near the lamp. 'There's something down there ahead of you.'

'I know.' He turned on another dim lamp. 'It's all these.' They walked cautiously towards him and then they saw, beyond him, standing on a long bench, row after row of birds. 'He must have been getting them ready to take them somewhere,' said Boris.

Jay suddenly realised what had made the noise. 'It was the light from the window,' he said. 'It was too bright and it made them flutter.'

'Full marks,' said Boris. 'When you told me

about those dim lamps I guessed that's what it was.'

Jay was looking at the rows of birds. 'But we can't take them all away,' he said. 'There's too many.'

'We'll have to hide them,' said Boris.

'But where?' Jay looked feverishly up and down the corridor. There were some cupboards, but they were too obvious. 'Where can we hide them?' he asked hopelessly, and Em suddenly darted forward saying something utterly stupid.

'Where's the best place to hide a leaf?' she said. 'In a forest, of course.' She couldn't remember where she'd read it, but she knew it was true. She went up to the revolving door and tugged at it. 'Thank goodness he forgot to lock it,' she murmured, and the trembling tree and swaying birds swung out of the museum into the corridor. 'Here's the place to hide the birds,' she said. 'Among the other birds.'

'Brilliant!' cried Boris and all three of them began to stack birds in the exhibition case, wedging them into position alongside the stuffed birds on branches or standing them on

the imitation grass on the floor.

'That's the last,' Em gasped, and stood back. But then she froze, because voices echoed in the museum outside and a moment later there was the rattle of a latch as someone opened the glass door of the exhibition case.

11

The Birds

'What do you think you're doing in there?'

The voice made them stiffen in the dark corridor.

'Come out!'

It was a voice that gave orders, deep and insulting, but a moment later they realised it was not meant for them. It came from the museum on the other side of the revolving door; nobody could know they were in the corridor.

It came again. 'Get out of there, man! You're wasting time!' It was the man from the Hill, and his voice was booming at someone else.

It was the Keeper who answered him. 'But I'm sure I didn't leave it like this,' he said, and he sounded so close he must have been standing inside the empty cabinet. The birds and the dead tree were still inside the corridor. 'I'm quite sure I left it closed,' said the Keeper.

'Closed? What do you mean, closed?' The

voice was heavy with anger. 'If you don't do something soon, Mr Bond, I'll tip the wink to my young man outside and your parents won't like what he does to them — young Jeremy has some very nasty habits.'

'I'm trying to tell you,' said the Keeper. 'The birds are in here.'

'It's an empty case! Do you take me for a fool!'

The sudden bark of anger made Em jump, and all three of them backed away. Their only hope of escape was the window, but it was shuttered, and now it was too late. The door began to revolve.

'What the devil are you up to!'

The voice roared and there was the sound of a struggle. Then the door jerked, suddenly revolved quickly, and the birds slid away out of sight.

The Keeper stood in front of them, blinking and panting and suddenly so startled to see them that he froze.

For a split second they gazed at each other in the dim light of the lamps while the man raged outside. But then, behind the Keeper, a new sound echoed in the museum. It began quite softly, but rose suddenly to such a pitch that the man's voice was drowned and lost.

The Keeper spun round and put his eye to the viewing slit. He gave a cry of surprise but they could see nothing until, unable to believe his eyes, he tugged open the window panel in the back of the cabinet. What they saw was nothing but a seething mass of beating wings.

Boris was the first to realise what was happening. 'It's the light!' he cried. 'The sunlight's on the birds!'

The setting sun streamed full into the cabinet and brought the birds to life. They crowded out with beating wings, brushing branches aside, thrusting at the glass door to push it wider, and sweeping out in a massive flying flock over and around the man who stood like a boulder in a flashing stream of bright feathers.

'How?' said the Keeper. 'How?' but they did not pause to explain. At any moment the man would recover.

'We've got to get out!' Em began to tug the Keeper towards the window where Jay and

Boris were pulling the shutters wide.

The Keeper pushed in front of them. 'They've got my parents in the square!' he yelled, and jumped from the ledge.

They scrambled after him but he was out of sight before they dropped into the alley. They ran until the crack of a shot split the air and made them crouch in the echoing passageway and look back. But no one was following them. They were alone.

'The shot came from the square,' said Jay and suddenly, sickeningly, they realised that was where the blond man was guarding the old couple. They left the alleyway and went forward on trembling legs and with fear clutching their stomachs.

They saw the man with the gun. He stood in the centre of the square, his legs apart, straddling a bird that was flapping at his feet. He paid it no attention. He was looking up at the front of the museum, concentrating, and then he raised his gun slowly, taking aim at something near the roof. They saw a glint of blue and green as a bird squeezed through the gap in an open window, and then he fired.

The jet of smoke and the roar of the shot battered their ears, and then the crash of falling glass as the whole window blew in. It was still tinkling down when his Chief came plunging down the steps yelling at him to stop, swearing at him for being an idiot.

He was trying to wrench the gun from the blond man's hands when a river of birds, as bright and glittering as a waterfall, came cascading out of the wrecked window and swirled in a torrent around the rooftops of the square.

But Em was looking for the Keeper. And then she saw him. He was crouching by the line of Trixies parked opposite the museum. She saw him reach up to a door handle and, as the tumult went on overhead, he tugged the door open and first his mother and then his father slid out and crawled away behind the line of gleaming bubbles.

The Chief's fury made the other man stagger back, but still they fought for the gun until the piercing scream of a police air patrol hovering overhead sent them diving into their Trixie and spinning out of the square.

The Keeper was the first to stand up. He

was helping his mother to her feet when they ran up to him.

'No harm done,' she said, brushing the knees of her orange suit.

'I'm not so sure about that,' said her husband, looking up. Birds were everywhere. A flock was wheeling overhead, others were strutting on the steps of the museum, and more still were fluttering about inside trying to find a way out. 'They're not much of a secret any more,' said old Mr Bond, looking at his son.

The Keeper smiled happily. 'Well, Dad,' he said, 'now that everybody knows about them, they're not much use to spies.'

'I hope you're satisfied, the pair of you,' said Mrs Bond, but her husband was looking towards the road leading out of the square.

'They won't get far in that stupid little Trixie they're driving, he said. 'Now if they'd had the sense to take my Lotus . . .' and Jay looked at Boris and then at Em and they all three began to laugh.